"Listen, listen!" I sat up, very straight. "We're all going to Heathfield, right?"

"Right." Keri nodded.

"'Cos it's the nearest," said Frizz.

"And the best!" said Keri. "Frensham's is huge and Clark's is a dump."

"We are not going to be separated," said Keri.

"No way!" said Lily.

We've been together ever since Reception. We've stayed together, through thick and thin. We've quarrelled, sometimes, and sat at different tables, and one year Keri didn't invite me and Frizzle to her birthday party and another year Lily hung out with Elinor Stoddart for a week or so, but always, in the end, we've got back together. We're the Gang of Four! Lily and Keri, Frizzle and me.

Also by Jean Ure
in the Girlfriends series

Girls Stick Together!
Girls Are Groovy!
Boys Are OK!

Orchard Black Apples

Get a Life
Just 16
Love is for Ever

ORCHARD BOOKS
96 Leonard Street
London EC2A 4XD
Orchard Books Australia
Unit 31/56 O'Riordan Street, Alexandria, NSW 2015
ISBN 1 84121 835 9
First published in Great Britain in 2002
A paperback original
Text © Jean Ure 2002
The right of Jean Ure to be identified as the author of
this work has been asserted by her in accordance with the
Copyright, Designs and Patents Act, 1988.
A CIP catalogue record for this book is available from the British Library.
5 7 9 10 8 6 4
Printed in Great Britain

Pink Knickers Aren't Cool!

Jean Ure

ORCHARD BOOKS

Chapter 1

"Honestly! Just look at that girl," said Keri.

In the middle of the playground, in full view of absolutely everyone, Jessamy Jones was standing on her head. Her legs were in the air, and her skirt had gone *flump!* all over her face.

"Showing off," I said.

"Don't worry," said Lily. "She'll fall over in a minute."

But she didn't. Worse luck! She went on standing there, upside down, surrounded by a group of admirers. All girls from our class. Jessamy Jones is in our class. *Unfortunately*. She is someone we hold in total contempt.

"Lily could do what she's doing," said Frizz.

"Yes, I could," said Lily. "But I wouldn't…not in front of everyone. Specially not in front of *boys.*"

It wasn't the boys' playground, but they can easily see into it from theirs.

"There's a gang of them watching right now," I said.

Lily sucked in her breath.

"Look at those knickers!" said Keri.

We looked. To be perfectly honest, they just seemed like ordinary knickers to me. I mean, she oughtn't to have been showing them, and she is a total grot, and I despise her utterly, but I couldn't actually see anything wrong with her knickers.

"*Pink,*" said Keri.

"Ugh! Groo!" said Lily.

Keri sniffed. "Well, but I ask you!"

So then I knew that pink knickers were naff. Keri is our authority on these things; she is really cool! She can even make school uniform seem like designer clothes. You should see her at weekends! Ten going on twenty, my mum says. If Keri tells us that pink knickers are naff, then we don't wear them. It's as simple as that.

I made a note to take out and lose ALL THE ONES

I had in my drawer at home. From this point on, I wouldn't be seen dead in them!

"Great galloping grandmothers! Now look at it," said Keri.

It was walking on its hands. Quite clever, really. But not more than Lily could have done! Lily just doesn't show off like some people. She is quite modest.

Suddenly, as we sat sourly watching, Frizz burst out with:

"Is pink bad?"

Oh, dear! Poor Frizz. She is so embarrassing at times. Lily giggled. Keri rolled her eyes.

"Get real!" she said.

"Well, but I don't see what's wrong with it," said Frizz. "I've got pink knickers." And she hoicked up her skirt to show us.

I suppose in a way it was quite brave. If I'd been wearing pink knickers I'd have died sooner than let on! But I sometimes seriously feel that Frizz is just a tiny bit young for her age. I guess it comes from having a mum and dad that are ancient. More like a nan and granddad, really. It makes them a bit old-fashioned so they think that at ten years old Frizz is still a young child. Instead of, as we keep reminding her, practically a teenager!

Keri leaned forward to hiss in her face.

"Take them off and bundle them up and throw them out with the rubbish!"

"But not now," I added, hastily.

Frizz was looking somewhat alarmed. "I couldn't throw them out! My mum would have a fit."

"Then don't tell her."

"But she'd wonder where they'd gone!"

"Just say you lost them," said Lily, kindly.

"But how?" wailed Frizz. "How do you lose knickers?"

"Don't ask," said Keri. "Oh, now look!" she said. "It's fallen over!"

"Serves it right," said Lily.

We all exulted like crazy, which probably sounds a bit small-minded but quite honestly she is not at all a nice person. Jessamy, I mean. Once when Frizz got stuck on a class reader while all the rest of us had moved on, she sneered and said she was a retard. And another time, when a boy called Ryan Spicer didn't ask to leave the room in time and left a trail of wee behind, she actually laughed at him. Not right there and then, because of our teacher being present; but afterwards, in the playground. She stood at the railings between our side and their side and she made these jeering remarks and people sniggered. I thought that was really mean.

I don't actually go for boys myself, none of us do. In our opinion they are quite stupid, always shouting out in class and thinking they are being clever when in fact they are just pathetic; but Ryan is not like the others. He tries to be. He pretends to swagger and bluster and be all loud and macho, but underneath he is quite a timid sort of person.

It was horrid of Jessamy to laugh at him. And at Frizz, just because she is not the brightest.

"To think," I said, "that we're going to have to spend the next *seven years* with it!"

"Ugh! Groo!" said Lily.

"Only if we stay on till seventeen," said Frizz, doing a bit of hasty fingerwork.

"Help! Help! When's the earliest you can leave?" I said.

"Sixteen, I *think*."

I went into a mock swoon. "I'll never survive! Having to see that in class every day!"

"Maybe it'll go to a different school," said Lily, hopefully.

"There isn't any different school!"

"Yes, there is," said Keri. "There's Frensham

Manor, there's Heathfield, there's Clark's—"

"Listen, listen!" I sat up, very straight. "We're all going to Heathfield, right?"

"Right." Keri nodded.

"'Cos it's the nearest," said Frizz.

"And the best!" said Keri. "Frensham's is huge and Clark's is a dump."

"Maybe that's where she'll go." Frizz giggled. "Just about suit her!"

"I don't care where she goes so long as it's not where we go," said Lily.

"But we are, definitely, all going to Heathfield," I said. "Aren't we?"

"Definitely," said Frizz; and she nodded her head up and down, very vigorously.

The others agreed.

"We are not going to be separated," said Keri.

"No way!" said Lily.

We've been together ever since Reception. We've stayed together, through thick and thin. We've quarrelled, sometimes, and sat at different tables, and one year Keri didn't invite me and Frizzle to her birthday party and another year Lily hung out with Elinor Stoddart for a week or so, but always, in the end, we've got back together. We're the Gang of

Four! Lily and Keri, Frizzle and me. Lily and Keri are best friends, and me and Frizz are best friends. But we are also all best friends with each other! We have had some really great times.

Maybe I should do a bit of explaining. Our names, first of all.

Lily's real name is Lilian, but she is always known as Lily. It really suits her as it is a flower name and Lily is rather like a flower, very slender and graceful. She, however, absolutely hates it! Both Lilian *and* Lily. She says that Lily Stubbs is not at all the right kind of name for a dancer (which is what she is going to be) and as soon as she possibly can she is going to change it. *Completely.* What to, she hasn't yet decided. Probably something romantic like Crystal, or Tatiana. Whatever it is, she will definitely be a dancer! She is determined on that. Lily is an extremely sweet person, always happy and full of fun, and never ever mean, but she has this streak in her, what Mum calls *a rod of steel*, meaning that she will not allow ANYTHING to get in the way of becoming a dancer. One day for sure she will be famous!

Keri is short for Kerianne; Kerianne Fox. Keri is the only one of us who actually likes her name. The rest of us all hate ours. But Keri likes most things about herself. I'm not saying she is conceited. Not really. But as she says, "If *you* don't like yourself, who else is going to?" This is something her mum and dad have taught her. It is for giving you confidence, of which I must say she has a LOT.

Frizz is just the opposite: she is not at all a confident sort of person. She never pushes herself forward or lays down the law. She is always trying to point out to us that Frizzell (which is her surname) is not pronounced Frizzle, it is pronounced Friz*elle*. But we still call her Frizzle! Or mostly Frizz. We have been doing it so long it would be difficult to stop. Her first name is Dawn, and as I said, she doesn't like it anyway.

Any more than I like mine!!! It is Polly, and I really, really *hate* it. A teacher we once had used to call me Polly Flinders, even though in fact it is Polly Roberts. My dad calls me Poll Doll, just to tease. My brother calls me Poll Doll to annoy. My brother is a very annoying sort of person. He is only eighteen months older than me but the way he carries on you'd think it was more like eighteen years. (Except that at the same time he is extremely childish in his behaviour, the same as most boys.)

What we look like

This is what we look like:

Face Shapes

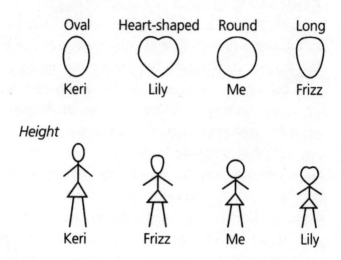

Height

Lily is tiny! She is also very dainty, with black eyes, black hair, cut short with a fringe, a teeny tilty nose and dimples when she smiles. My mum once said she looks like a little doll. She is really cute!

Keri is tall and quite big, by which I mean she has Big Bones. She is not fat! She has lovely long legs that go on for simply ever, and gorgeous red hair that froths and foams and sprays all about in little tendrils.

Now and again the boys try calling her Carrots, or Carrot Top, but she just withers them with this LOOK. Withering is the sort of thing you can do when you're like Keri. I couldn't wither anyone if I tried! Keri doesn't have to try; it just comes naturally.

Frizz is also quite tall; but unlike Keri she is not big-boned. She is rather soft and pillowy. Mrs Arkle, our class teacher, says that she has not yet "firmed up". I think perhaps this is because she is not very athletic. Lily has her dancing, and Keri is on the netball team, and even I walk our dog, Bundle, up to the park every day; but what Frizz likes to do is help her mum and dad in the shop. Between you and me, I think she eats too much chocolate and too many crisps! I expect I would do the same if my mum and dad owned a shop. How could you help it???

Frizzle's hair is dark brown and shoulder length, and she has a brace on her teeth and rather a long nose. A boy called Vinny Hassett, a particularly horrible sort of boy, once said that Frizzle's nose looked like a door knocker. He tweaked it and went "Knock, knock!" and made Frizz cry. People can sometimes be quite unkind to Frizz; I don't know why. She just seems to be that sort of person. It is true that she is not clever, and nor is she particularly pretty, but she is funny and generous and my best *best* friend, and I hate it when people are nasty to her.

Now I suppose I will have to describe me, and that is difficult as I am extremely nondescript. Alas! My hair, for instance, is brownish, and shortish, and curlyish. My face is roundish, my eyes are roundish, my cheeks are roundish. I am not tall (*sigh*) but on the other hand I am not as short as some people. I am definitely not thin (*double sigh*) but I am not fat, either. Just medium. Somewhere in between. Oh, and at the moment – alas, again! – I wear glasses. I say "at the moment" because one day I am going to have contact lenses. I hate wearing glasses! They make you look learned, like a boffin.

When I have my contact lenses, they are going to be *green*. I would love to have green eyes! I would love to be tall! I would love to have long blond *straight* hair that looks as if it has been ironed. I would love to be called Jade. I would love to have skin that was golden brown, like honey. (Instead of pale pink, like a prawn.)

Dream on!

The only thing I am quite proud of is my teeth, which may sound an odd sort of thing to be proud of. I mean, teeth are not like hair or eyes. No one ever says, "What beautiful teeth that girl has" or "I wish I could have teeth like that". Most people just don't even notice. But one time when I had to go to the dentist's for a check up – just a check up! no fillings; I hardly ever have to have fillings – the dentist told Mum that I was lucky. He said I had really good teeth.

"Lovely and straight," he said. He told me to look after them 'cos they were teeth to be proud of! So now, if ever I am having my photo taken or, like, saying hello to someone, I grin like crazy. You can't do it all the time or people would think there was something wrong with you, but I do it as often as I can. After all, it is no different, really, from Lily twizzling her legs about or Keri flicking her hair.

As the bell rang for afternoon class, and we trooped back across the playground, Frizz tucked her arm into mine and whispered, "We will all go to Heathfield, won't we?"

I said, "Of course we will!"

Frensham's was too big, and Clark's was a dump. Of course we would all go to Heathfield!

"We're the Gang of Four," I said.

"Friends for ever," said Frizz.

Friends for ever. No one was going to separate *us*!

Chapter 2

At the end of school, Keri and Lily are always picked up by their mums. Lily is driven off to her dancing class. She has classes four times a week! She does tap and ballet, disco and salsa. And then on Saturdays she does drama. She is really dedicated!

Keri goes off with her mum in their BIG car to their BIG house in The Glades. The Glades is where all the posh people live. The houses are, like, separated; not all stuck together so that your mum is forever yelling at you to "Stop making that noise, you'll upset the neighbours!" Keri can make as much noise as she likes and no one, probably, would ever complain. When you are in her garden you wouldn't even know that she has any neighbours. Whereas in my garden you can look over the fence and see Mrs Pritchett-from-next-door's washing hanging on the line – pink knickers! – Big ones! – and hear whenever Mr Deacon on the other side is watching the telly because he is deaf and has it really LOUD.

Keri's mum and dad are seriously rich. Not rich like the Queen, or the Spice Girls, but richer than any of our mums and dads. This is how come she gets to have ace parties with big stripy tents in the back garden, and discos. We couldn't get a big stripy tent in our back garden! Frizz doesn't even have a garden. Lily does, but it is about the size of a biscuit tin.

Lily's mum has to do two different jobs to pay for all her dancing lessons. During the day she is a school dinner lady, and in the evening she cleans people's offices. Lily said that when she is famous she is going to buy a house like Keri's for her mum and dad to live in and they are not going to work again, ever. Not unless they want to!

Me and Frizz are the only two that are not met after school. We always walk down the hill together to

Bridge Street, and along Bridge Street until we come to The Bridge Newsagent, which is where Frizzle lives. There is a sweet little tiny door at the side of the shop with these very narrow stairs behind it. At the top of the stairs is a dear little flat, very old and quaint, with an attic bedroom high up in the roof for Frizz. It is great fun staying with Frizz and sleeping in the attic. It has a little old fireplace and mantelpiece and is where the poor servant used to sleep in olden days. Me and Frizz lie in bed and stare up at the stars through her skylight window and imagine what it must have been like to be a servant. Today we see the planes zooming overhead on their way to Heathrow Airport. Sometimes in winter we see snowflakes falling, or hear the rain splatting down and watch it bouncing off the glass while we snuggle up all safe and cosy below. I would love to have an attic bedroom like Frizzle's!

There is a bus stop right outside the shop, so Frizz always waits with me until the bus arrives. Usually her mum pops out and gives us a Twix or a packet of crisps. Then I am on the bus and heading for home, a journey which takes perhaps twenty minutes. I like travelling on the bus by myself! It makes me feel responsible, and grown-up. I think it is far better than being taken everywhere by your mum. Well, anyway, that is my opinion.

The very same day that we all made our vow about going to Heathfield together, I got home and had a bit of a shock. Mum said, "Tell me, Polly! How would you feel about trying for the High School?"

I said, "*High* School?" in a wittering sort of way. I mean, I'd heard perfectly well what she'd said.

"Yes! How about it?" said Mum.

"I don't want to go to the High School!" I wailed. "We're all going to Heathfield!"

The High School is our local posh school. All girls, and dead brainy.

"I'd never get in there," I said.

"Why not?" said Mum. "How do you know?"

I said, "'Cos I wouldn't!"

"You don't know till you try," said Mum. "After all, Craig got into King Henry's."

Craig is my brother. And King Henry's is our other posh school. All boys. Also dead brainy. My brother is a real boffin! He is going to be a nuclear physicist. (Whatever that is.)

"If he can do it—" said Mum.

"He got a scholarship," I said.

"Well," said Mum, "and so might you!"

"I wouldn't," I said. "I'm not a boffin!"

Mum said, "Polly, don't sell yourself short. You may be cleverer that you think."

I didn't want to be cleverer than I thought! I didn't want to go to the High School! I just wanted to be me and go to Heathfield.

I said this to Mum and she sighed and shook her head; and then Craig came clumping in, in his foul purple uniform. Purple blazers with *bright yellow stripes.* Ugh! Groo. Uniforms are so yucky. At some schools you can wear whatever you like.

What with Craig clattering and clanging all about the kitchen, and Bundle, our pooch, shouting in his loud doggy voice and bouncing up and down – Mum always says that Craig incites him to riot – we didn't get to talk about the High School any more. Thank goodness!

It is alarming when your mum and dad take these ideas into their heads. You have to squash them *immediately*, before they start getting all enthusiastic. If they get enthusiastic and then you say, "No, I don't want to" they fall into a dudgeon, which is like very offended and hurt. "Oh, but why ever not?" they go and "Why couldn't you say so before?" they go. They make you feel really guilty. So I was glad I had squashed it before it could go too far.

All the same, it had given me something to worry about. When I met up with Frizzle outside the shop next morning, I said, "We've got to talk! We've got to have a meeting!"

"About what?" said Frizzle.

"We've got to swear an oath," I said.

I wouldn't tell her any more; not until break time when we were all together in our secret place, which is behind the gardening shed in the corner of the playground. We discovered one day that there was just enough room between the shed and the wall for us to squeeze in. Two of us hoist ourselves up and sit on the wall – Keri and Frizz, being the two tallest – while me and Lily squat on upturned flower pots. It's totally and absolutely guaranteed one hundred per cent private! No one knows about it except us. Well, if they do they certainly can't come pushing in while we are there. There isn't so much as a spare centimetre of space!

"OK, so what's the big emergency?" said Keri, when we were all in position.

"I was thinking," I said. "What we talked about the other day…about us all going to Heathfield. We ought to swear an oath!"

"You mean, like a blood oath?" said Lily.

"Yes, and then it's sealed and there's nothing anyone can do to separate us."

Keri nodded. "Yes. That's good!"

I could feel myself glowing. Keri is usually the one to have all the ideas. If she approved of it, it had to be good!

"So what happens?" said Frizz. "How do we do it?"

"First of all we have to work out what we're going to swear."

"Get a piece of paper!" Keri dived bossily into her bag and hauled out her rough book. Then she dived back again and came out with a pen. "Right! We'll say...what shall we say? *I swear—*"

"That we're all going to Heathfield," said Frizz.

"No! I know!" Lily bounced on her flower pot. *"We swear to stay together, come what may, for better or for worse, all the time we're still at school."*

"Friends for ever!" added Frizz.

"Friends for ever," agreed Lily.

"Friends for ever, but I've got an idea, I've got an idea!" I bounced, excitedly. "We could make a poem! We could say...

"We swear to stay together
All the time we're still at school.

For better or for worse
'Cos that's our rule!"

"Brilliant." Keri scribbled in her rough book. "How did it go? *We swear to stay together—*"

I repeated it for her and she wrote it out, four times. One for each of us.

"You're our poet," beamed Frizz.

I am rather good at writing poetry, I must admit.

"What about the blood bit?" said Keri.

There was a silence as we thought about this.

"I've got a safety pin," said Lily.

"Ugh!" Frizz squirmed.

Lily reached into her bag and brought out this pin that was about the size of a dagger, practically. I saw Frizz's eyes go like saucers.

"What's that for?" I shrieked.

Lily explained that it had come off one of her mum's skirts that she didn't wear any more.

"I liked it, so I kept it."

"But what is it *for*?" said Keri.

"For jabbing into fingers and drawing blood!" screeched Lily, swooping with her pin.

Frizz gave a little squeal. "I'm not jabbing my finger!"

"So how are you going to get blood?"

"I've got a scab I could pick," said Frizz.

"I could try picking my nose," I said. "Sometimes when I do that it sets it off bleeding."

"Oh! Yuck!" cried Lily. "That's disgusting!"

"I'm not picking my nose," said Keri. "And I haven't got a scab, and I'm certainly not sticking that great thing in myself!"

"So how are we supposed to swear a blood oath without any blood?" said Lily.

"We'll swear a spit oath!"

It was Keri's idea. She said that spit was every bit as good as blood, and didn't involve any jabbing or picking.

We thought that was pretty neat. Lily took her yoghurt from out of her lunch box and ate it, then wiped the pot clean with a paper hanky and very solemnly (except for Frizz, who giggled) we all spat into it – "Great gobbets," instructed Keri, "so's it can be mixed up" – and Lily swizzled it around with a pencil. Then one by one we dipped our fingers and recited the oath:

"We swear to stay together
All the time we're still at school.

For better or for worse
'Cos that's our rule!"

After which we licked our fingers.
Gross!
But we had done it. No one could part us now.

Chapter 3

The term jogged on, which is what terms mostly seem to do. Sometimes they drag a bit, and sometimes they gallop, but on the whole I would say that they just jog.

These are some of the things that happened.

No. 1. A girl called Melanie Philpotts got into a fight with a girl called Darcie White, and broke her finger. *She* said Darcie twisted it, though Darcie said she didn't. Darcie said it was all Melanie's fault, because (she said) Melanie had bitten her. Except in that case, as Keri pointed out, there would surely have been teeth marks. Which there weren't! If there had've been, Darcie would have gone round showing them to everyone.

It was all a great mystery and they both got told off. Oh, and Melanie had to go to the hospital and came into school the next day with her arm in a sling. I really envied her that! I would love to have my arm in a sling. Very rrrrromantic! Well, I think so. Frizz disagrees. She says that in fact it would be extremely inconvenient and probably painful, as well; but Frizz is not noted for her imagination. She is very down to earth.

Happening No. 2. Our dog Bundle fell in love with a dear little sweet darling spaniel that lives up the road. He suffered the most terrible pangs! He sat in the garden and howled all day long. It was so sad! I said to Mum, "He loves her! He just wants to be with her."

Mum said, "Well, he can't! He's far too young and scatty to be a dad."

"You mean, they might have *puppies*?" I said.

"I'm sure they would!" said Mum.

Mum seemed to think this would be a bad thing, but I think it would be great. I would love to have a puppy! Especially one of Bundle's. He is just so cute, and the spaniel is so pretty, they would be adorable!

But Mum said no way, and poor Bundle howled and fretted for a whole week. I couldn't even take him for walks because he just sat down outside the gate of number ten and refused to move. Craig had to come with me so that he could pick him up and carry him.

In the end he got over it, Bundle I mean, and decided that perhaps he wasn't in love after all. Mum said thank goodness for that! Now maybe life could get back to normal. Which it did.

Happening No. 3. Mum gave away my favourite, favourite, FAVOURITE top without asking me. She is always doing this! Giving my things away. She said, "Oh, by the way, Polly, the lady from Oxfam called round and I gave her a load of stuff, including some of your old clothes."

Knowing Mum, I shrieked, "Which ones?"

"Just things you don't wear any more," said Mum.

I immediately raced upstairs to check. "Where is my top?" I bellowed. "*Mum! Where is my top?*"

"If you're talking about the one with the flowers—" said Mum.

"Where's it gone?" I howled.

"Polly, it was far too small for you," said Mum. "You haven't been able to get into it for months!"

But that is not the point. It was *mine*. Mum has no

right to give away things that are mine! For all she knows I might suddenly start shrinking and be able to get into them again.

I said this to her and she said, "I have never heard of anyone your age shrinking."

I said, "There's always a first time," and went off in a huff.

What Mum didn't seem to realise was that you don't just chuck things out 'cos they're old or they don't fit you any more. They're, like, a part of you. Like my dolls that she gave away. I *know* I was too old to play with them, but it was horrid when they weren't there any more. I would have given them away, in time; I just wasn't ready for it yet. Same with my top. It's so mean of Mum to do these things!

She obviously felt guilty 'cos the very next day she took me into town and said that I had better choose a new one for myself. So I did. Black, with orange feathery bits! The sort of thing that normally Mum would say was not suitable, only this time she didn't dare! She let me have it. Hooray!

Happening No. 4. Jessamy Jones got chosen to be part of some gymnastics team. All the girls in our class that think she's, like, the cat's whiskers, went "Oooh" and "Aaah" and "Jessamy, you're so clever!" Jessamy pranced and preened and tossed her hair – it is long and silvery and she just *loves* to toss it – until we all felt positively sick.

Lily could have been in the gym team if she'd wanted; she's just as good as Jessamy. But Lily has more important things to do! Like she has her dancing exams to work for. One day Lily is going to be *famous*.

Horrible thought: maybe Jessamy will also be famous??? Maybe she will win gold medals at the next Olympics? Oh, no! *Please!* I couldn't bear it.

But I don't think it will happen. She's not dedicated enough. She just likes to show off.

Happening No. 5. Half term! Half term was brilliant as me and Frizz stayed at each other's places. Frizz stayed with me for two days, then I stayed with her. Craig went off camping with Dad, and that was even more brilliant! He can be such a nuisance when Frizz is here. He knows that she is easy to embarrass and so he is always saying and doing things to make her blush. Like he'll say, "Oops! Pardon my underpants!" (his latest stupid phrase) just for the fun of seeing her cheeks turn scarlet. Boys are *so* idiotic.

It was quite a relief, for once, to be on our own. It meant for instance that we could go to and from the bathroom in our nighties without any danger of Craig

– or Dad! – suddenly appearing. I mean, it doesn't bother me as I am used to it, but poor Frizz is ever so bashful.

After she stayed with me, I went to stay with her. There is only room for one tiny little bed in her tiny little attic, so we have to share, but we don't mind. We take it in turns to be the one who sleeps on the inside, next to the wall. The one who sleeps on the inside gets *squashed*; but the one who sleeps on the outside has been known to fall out – *bump!* – onto the floor, in the middle of the night. Fortunately there is a soft fluffy rug there, so it is not too painful!

One of the best things about staying with Frizz is that I get to help in the shop. I really love to do this! I love to take people's money and open the till and count out the change. It is like playing at supermarkets when I was little. Except better, because it's real!

Happening No. 6. We all met up at Keri's place and Keri's mum drove us to the Silver Glades ice rink, where Keri goes once a week to do her ice skating. Keri is into ice skating in a big way. (She is also into netball, softball, tennis, rounders, and swimming. Oh, and running and jumping, as well. And skiing! She is terrifically sporty.)

Me and Frizz had never been skating before and

were not very good at it. I suppose it is true to say that we are not at all athletic. But it was fun staggering about and clutching at each other and giggling as we fell over, which we did quite a lot!

Lily was wearing a tiny little short red skirt and a black top with red trimming. She just looked *so* cute! She had only been skating once before but she was soon skimming across the ice and doing twizzly bits and turns and didn't fall over once. I expect it is her dance training, or else she just has naturally perfect balance, like some people have perfect pitch. (But not me! Whenever I try singing, Craig puts his fingers in his ears and Bundle starts to howl. I try pretending that he is just joining in, but most likely it is because he is in pain.)

Keri, of course, being a practised skater, can do all kinds of exciting things. Great leaps and spins and flying about on one leg. She is hugely athletic, but Lily is more graceful.

After the ice skating, Keri's mum took us to tea in a posh sort of tea room with real waitresses all dressed in black, with frilly caps. Dead classy! Me and Frizz ate gorgeous sticky meringues the size of giant puffballs. Two each! Keri had something Italian that I can't remember the name of, but Lily just ate...bread and butter! I can't imagine why, as she certainly doesn't need to slim, but she said it was what she wanted.

Happening No. 7. We all met up next day and mooched round the shopping centre to spend what was left of our holiday money. About 50p, in my case! Poor old Frizz didn't have any at all. She gets less than the rest of us; even less than Lily. Keri, who gets a vast amount, insisted on treating her to a Coke and some French fries. She said, "We're friends! This is the sort of things that friends do."

It's funny, with Keri. There are times when she can be a right pain, but other times she is just so loyal, and so generous, you forget about her bumptious bossiness and the way she always seems to take over. She doesn't do it on purpose, I don't think; she just has this tremendously forceful personality.

Anyway, that was half term. Three days later, we went back to school and Vinny Hassett had a nose bleed all over everything, including me. He shook his head and it all splatted and splodged. Ugh! Groo! I turned to Lily, who was sitting next to me, and said, "It'd be all right if I wanted to swear a blood oath with him…but I don't!"

I thought that Lily looked a bit odd when I said this. I decided that it was most probably the sight of blood, making her feel faint. It was only later I discovered the true reason. At the time I was too busy scrubbing myself with a paper hanky, then Mrs Arkle said that I had better go to the cloakroom and wash my face, and by the time I got back the bell had rung for break.

Lily was really quiet all through that break time. She is normally very bright and sparky, always wanting to dart about and do things.

"Let's make a wheelie," said Frizz.

A wheelie is where we all link arms and go wheeling off across the playground, in a line. If people get in our way, we simply *wheel* around them! Whatever we do, we don't break the line. That is the whole point of it. So we made our wheelie and went wheeling off, but somehow you could just tell that Lily's heart wasn't in it. It is always her and me on the outside. We are the ones who set the wheel in motion. But today it was me that was doing all the wheeling; Lily was just following. Even Keri noticed it. I mean usually, as a rule, she doesn't notice anything very much unless it's like Jessamy showing off her knickers. That is the sort of thing that Keri notices. But not if it's just someone being a bit quiet, like Lily was.

That day, she noticed. She kept making these impatient tutting noises and going, "*Move* it, *move* it!" But it was Frizz who spoke out first.

"Are you all right?" she said.

"Me? Yes. Why?" said Lily.

"Just wondered," said Frizz.

"I'm perfectly all right," said Lily.

"Then why aren't you doing anything?" demanded Keri. "You're not *doing* anything. Move it, move it!"

So Lily immediately wheeled away to the right and led us in a huge wheelie round Jessamy Jones and her gang.

"Way to go!" yelled Keri.

"Way to go!" yelled me and Frizz.

"Way to go!" yelled Lily.

She was making like everything was normal, but somehow you could just tell that her heart wasn't in it. And then it was like she couldn't keep it to herself any more. As the bell rang for the end of break, and we wheeled back across the playground, she hissed, "We've got to have a meeting!"

I don't know why, but this feeling of doom came upon me. I think a similar feeling must have come upon Frizz.

"Why?" she said; and her face looked all pale. "What's happened?"

"Tell you later," said Lily. She broke away and went

running ahead of us into school.

"Something's happened," said Frizz.

"Hmm…" Keri rubbed a finger across her forehead. I pushed my glasses up my nose. What could it be? And why did I have this feeling that it was something bad?

We had to wait till after lunch to find out. Lily wouldn't tell us in the dining hall. We kept on at her, but she just shook her head and said, "Not yet!"

As soon as we'd finished we rushed to our secret hiding place and squeeeeeeezed ourselves in.

"Right!" Keri sat upright on the wall. "What is it? Tell! Don't keep us in suspense!"

"Well…" Lily forked her fingers into her fringe, bristling it up like a porcupine. "The thing is—"

"What?" said Keri.

"The thing is," gabbled Lily, "I've been offered a place at Rosemount!"

There was a stunned silence. Rosemount is a dance school; very big and famous. People go there from all over.

"But I thought they'd turned you down!" I said.

Lily nodded; sort of happily-unhappily, both at the same time.

"So did I!"

She'd gone for an audition ages ago, long before

41

we'd even thought of swearing our blood oath. She'd told us about the letter they'd written, saying how they couldn't offer her a place "at this moment". Maybe later, she could apply again. Lily had sort of resigned herself to not going until she was sixteen. She was *definitely going to go*. But she was going to have to wait.

"So what's made them change their minds?" I said.

Lily beamed, then hastily pulled her lips back into a straight line. "They put me on a waiting list...if anyone dropped out, they'd reconsider. And someone did. And they have. And now I'm going there!"

This time she couldn't stop herself. The beam spread upwards from her lips, to her cheeks, to her nose. Her cheeks went all dimply and her nose crinkled.

"What about our spit oath?" said Frizz. She sounded bewildered. The beam disappeared.

"I'm sorry," whispered Lily. "I wouldn't have taken it if I'd known!"

I expect we should have congratulated her, but we were just, like, in a state of shock. It was only a few weeks ago that we'd all dipped our fingers in each other's spit and solemnly sworn to be true. To stay together.

"For better or for worse," said Frizz.

Lily hung her head.

"Well!" Keri slid slowly down off the wall. "It can't be helped. She can't be expected to turn it down."

I agreed that she couldn't.

"I mean, if she wants to be famous—"

"I just want to dance," muttered Lily.

"You want to be famous," said Keri. "*We* want you to be famous! Don't we?"

She turned to me and Frizz.

I said, "Yes. Of course we do!" Frizz nodded, a bit uncertainly.

"I'm really sorry," whispered Lily.

"It's all right," said Keri. "We understand! Your dancing has to come first." She looked rather sternly at me and Frizz. "It's not like it's anything new," she said. "We've always known that Lily is *dedicated*."

Frizz swallowed. "Some people don't go to dance school till they're older," she said. "Like when they leave school, or something. Why couldn't you wait till then?"

"'Cos she doesn't want to wait till then! She wants

43

to go now. We ought to be congratulating her," said Keri. "Not going on at her."

Of course me and Frizz immediately said well done and congratulations.

"I hope you enjoy it," said Frizz.

"I will! I know I will!" said Lily. "It's what I've always always wanted. But I'm going to miss you terribly!"

"We're going to miss you," said Frizz.

Keri would miss her even more than me and Frizz. It's always been me and Frizz, Lily and Keri. But Keri is not the sort of person to sit down and weep over what can't be helped. She is very get-up-and-go.

"It's not as if it's in London or anything," she said. "It's only just up the road! We'll still be able to see each other."

But it wouldn't be the same, and we all knew it.

Chapter 4

When I got home that afternoon I told Mum about Lily going to Rosemount.

"Oh, that is good news!" said Mum.

Good news??? I suppose she meant for Lily. It wasn't for the rest of us! We'd been the Gang of Four almost ever since I could remember. I stayed silent.

"Oh, Polly!" said Mum. "You mustn't be selfish…think of Lily! It must be so wonderful for her. She must be so excited!"

I heaved a sigh. "I s'ppose so."

"It's everything she's ever dreamed of," said Mum.

"It's everything she's worked for! Try not to begrudge it."

"I don't begrudge it," I said. "I'm very happy for her. I am! Honestly! But it's all going to be different."

"I'm afraid that would happen anyway," said Mum. "You're all growing up, you're all going to go your separate ways."

"Not for years and years," I said. "We were all going to go to Heathfield together. We made a pact. We swore an oath!"

"Polly." Mum turned from the table, where she'd been chopping things on her chopping board. "There's something I've been meaning to say to you. Y—"

At this point the door bell rang.

"Oh, bother!" said Mum. "Who can that be? Polly, go and see who it is, there's a good girl."

Who it was was Mrs Pritchett. Her from next door. With the big knickers! She stood on the step looking like a withered grape, with her lips all pursed and her cheeks sucked in. I thought, "Uh, oh! Trouble!"

"Mum!" I yelled. "It's Mrs Pritchett!"

"Well, ask her in," said Mum. "Don't leave her standing there!"

Mrs Pritchett had come to complain. She is always coming to complain. (Unlike Mr Deacon on the other side. He is a *dear* old man, even if he does keep me awake with his television set.) Usually what Mrs Pritchett comes to complain about is me and Craig making too much noise or kicking footballs into her garden. This time it was about Bundle, barking at her cat. Poor little innocent dog! He didn't mean any harm.

"It's what dogs do," said Craig, when Mum had apologised and Mrs Pritchett had gone stalking back to her own place, all stiff and self-righteous. "It's what they're programmed to do."

"Yes," I said, "he can't help it…he sees a cat and a bark comes over him."

For once me and Craig were in agreement. It doesn't happen very often! But Bundle is *our* dog, his and mine. He was a joint Easter present from Mum and Dad, and we love him to bits. Both of us!

"It's not so much the barking," said Mum, "as the jumping up and down and battering the fence. That fence is going to collapse one of these days, and it'll be us that have to pay for it!"

"Well, the cat shouldn't sit there if it doesn't want to be barked at," said Craig. "It only does it to annoy."

"And anyway," I said, "what right's it got to sit on our fence?"

"It's not our fence." said Mum, "It's Mrs Pritchett's."

"So why should we have to pay for it?" said Craig. "If it's not ours?"

"Because it's our dog that's battering it!" snapped Mum. She snatched up her chopping knife and began to chop, very fast and furious, at a carrot. "Where was I? We were talking about something! What was it?"

But Mum couldn't remember, and neither could I. I was too worried about poor Bundle, in case he got into trouble for battering the fence.

"I'm going to take him for a walk," I said. "Then he'll be too tired to batter."

"A good idea," said Mum. "Get him out from under my feet!"

Next day at school it seemed like everyone had heard about Lily going to Rosemount. I don't know how it got out, but things always do. You can't have any secrets, in our school. Not that it was a secret, I suppose; not any more.

The only good thing about it, it put Jessamy Jones's nose out of joint. You could practically see it bending. Her nose, I mean.

"I thought they'd turned you down," she said.

She'd been *really* pleased when that had happened. She'd said things like, "Oh, what a shame!" and "Please don't be upset, I'm sure you'll get in somewhere else" and you'd just known that she didn't mean a single word. She'd smiled so broadly she'd almost split her face. Now her nose was bending, and serve her right!

"I thought you'd tried once and they'd said no?"

"They never said *no*," said Keri. "They put her on a waiting list."

Jessamy said, "What's that supposed to mean?"

"Means if someone falls out you get to have their place."

"And someone *did* fall out," said Frizz.

"So now," I said, "she's going there!"

"So there," added Keri.

Even though we hated the thought of Lily not being with us any more, we weren't just going to stand around and let Jessamy Jones stamp all over her.

Jessamy's lip curled.

"You mean she wasn't their first choice," she said.

Honestly! You see what I mean about the girl? There are some people that should be squashed, and

49

stuffed into cushions, and *sat* upon. And Jessamy is one of them!

Fortunately not everyone in our class is as hateful as her. Melanie Philpotts said, "Anyone who gets into Rosemount has to be really good. It's one of the top dance schools in the country." She said that she knew this because her auntie was a dancer.

"And the only reaon she wasn't their first choice was because she was too young," added Keri. "Everybody else was already eleven."

I saw Lily looking at Keri gratefully. Then I looked at Keri. This was the first I'd heard! Was it true? Or was it something she'd just made up?

Something she'd just made up! I was sure of it! Lily looked as surprised as anyone. Luckily, Jessamy didn't notice.

"Being accepted when you're only ten," said Keri, "is practically unheard of. It's practically next door to genius. So there!"

Jessamy tossed her head so that her hair went flowing back like a great silvery curtain. It is one of her more annoying habits. Look at me! Look at my hair! Look how beautiful it is! *Stupid*. Showing off.

"When I get to Heathfield," she said, "I'm going to

join the gym club. They've got a brilliant gym club at Heathfield! They're just waiting for me to go there."

"How do you know?" said Keri.

Jessamy gave this little superior smirk. (Another of her annoying habits.)

"My cousin's there and she's told them about me. They want me on their gym team. They have one of the *best* gym teams…they came third in the Southern Counties last year."

There simply isn't any stopping her. She is totally *unsquashable.*

But ha ha! So is Keri. Especially when one of us is being got at.

"Huh! *Well.* That showed her," she said, as Jessamy went self-importantly stomping over to her table. "Now she knows you were only *ten.*"

"But so was everybody else!" hissed Lily.

"Yes, but some would have been nearly eleven," said Keri. "You weren't! And anyway, just shut up," she added. "You're going to be a star!"

At break time we mooched round the playground together. Jessamy was out there, showing off as usual. We watched for a moment in sour silence.

"Did you hear what she said, about going to

Heathfield?" said Frizz. "I didn't know *she* was going there!"

Somehow we'd all imagined that once we hit year seven we'd be free of her. I don't know why. What Mum would call "wishful thinking", I suppose.

"Hey, listen! Maybe we should all go somewhere else?" I said.

"I'm not going to Frensham's!" said Keri. "It's *huge*. And I'm not going to Clark's. Clark's is a *dump*."

We mooched on, in glum silence.

"I feel so guilty," said Lily.

"What for?" said Keri. "It's not your fault."

"No," said Lily, "but I'd feel a whole lot better if I knew you weren't going to be stuck with *her*!"

I groaned to Mum about it when I got home.

"That awful girl, that horrible Jessamy...she's going to Heathfield!"

"Isn't that where a lot of people will be going?" said Mum.

"Yes, but we'd hoped we were going to get away from her!"

"Oh, come on," said Mum, "she can't be as bad as all that."

"She can be. She is! She's hateful!"

"Well, maybe you won't have to be with her," said Mum.

"I will," I said, "I've just told you…she's going to Heathfield!"

"So maybe you'll be going somewhere else," said Mum.

"What?" I stopped in my tracks, half way across the kitchen with Bundle's lead. "Where? Where else could I go?"

"It's what I was trying to tell you yesterday afternoon, but Mrs Pritchett called and put it right out of my head. Do you remember we talked about you trying for the High School?"

I felt all the blood go oozing out of my cheeks and trickling off somewhere else. Down to my toes, from the feel of things. There certainly wasn't any left in the top half of my body. Or if there was, it had turned to water. I didn't want to go to the High School! I wanted to stay with my friends!

"Mum," I wailed, "we talked about this before!"

"There can't be any harm in just trying," pleaded Mum. "Just go and sit the entrance exam and see how you get on. Just out of interest."

"But there isn't any *point*. I don't want to go there!"

"It's a very good school," said Mum.

"So's Heathfield!" I said.

"Yes, it is," agreed Mum, "and I'd be quite happy if you went to Heathfield. But just think! If you went to the High School it would be all girls!"

She knows I don't like boys.

"And smaller classes," said Mum. "No danger of getting swallowed up."

That's another thing: she knows I am sometimes a bit silly and shy. Well, timid. Like at the end of Year Six when we have to stand up and speak for a whole minute in front of all the school. Some people just love it! People like Keri and Jessamy; they were really looking forward to it. I was already shrivelling.

"I just feel," said Mum, "that it would be a better environment for you. But if you don't get in, you don't get in. Nothing to worry about! No harm done."

I wasn't worried about *not* getting in. I was worried in case I *did*!

"I'd have to have a scholarship," I said, "wouldn't I?"

"Well – yes," admitted Mum. "I'm afraid we don't have the money to pay for you."

Relief! I let out my breath in a big whooooosh. I'd never get a scholarship!

"So, do you think it might be fun just to try?" said Mum.

"Not really," I said. "I think it would be silly and a waste of time 'cos I'll never ever get a scholarship. Even if I did, I wouldn't want to go there!"

"But you wouldn't mind trying?" said Mum. "Just for me?"

"It's *pointless*," I said.

"But you'll do it?"

What can you say when your mum keeps on at you? I mumbled that I would do it for her but I still thought it was a waste of time.

"Polly, don't say that!" said Mum. "You don't know!" And then she broke it to me: they'd already filled in all the forms and been given the date for the exam. The date for the exam was – two weeks' time!

I shrieked, "*Mum!*"

"We just heard this morning," said Mum.

She was so excited! I wasn't. I was full of glummest gloom and despair. It is very terrible when your mum and dad behave like this. Going behind your back and suddenly springing it on you. Even if I wasn't going to get a scholarship, I'd still have all the horrible hassle of taking the exam.

"I'm only thinking what's best for you," said Mum.

To which I replied "Huh!" in tones of deep disgruntlement.

"Is it the High School?" said Craig, bursting through the door. My brother always bursts. He has no idea how to come into rooms like a normal person. I sometimes seriously wonder if he *is* a normal person.

"You'll like it there," he said. "Jobsy's sister goes there." Jobsy is his best friend. His real name is Kevin Jobson. "All the teachers are lesbians and unmarried mothers."

"Craig!" Mum took a swipe at him with a tea towel. "Don't be so ridiculous!"

"They are," insisted Craig. "Jobsy's sister told him."

"Then Jobsy's sister ought to know better! Take no notice of him, Polly. He's just being silly."

"Makes no difference to me," I said. I clipped Bundle's lead on and we hurtled across the kitchen to the back door. "Shan't be going there anyway."

Craig said, "Why not?"

"'Cos I won't get a scholarship!" I yelled, as me and Bundle flew through the door.

"Course you will," said Craig. "Easy peasy!"

Chapter 5

Next day I was cudgelling my brain, thinking how I could break the news to the rest of the gang. I didn't want to call a meeting. We only did that in emergencies, or for something really important. Frizz would get all alarmed and upset, and it would be totally *unnecessary* since I was only going to take the entrance exam. Not go to the school!

I thought for a bit that perhaps I wouldn't even bother to mention it; but we always tell each other things, specially me and Frizz. We don't have secrets. She would be really hurt if she somehow got to find out and I hadn't said anything.

At break we went into the playground. Frizz wanted to play wheelies but Keri said she was sick of wheelies. She said, "I've grown out of all that!"

Frizz's face fell. She is ever so easily crushed! Normally I would have stuck up for her. I would have said, for instance, that doing wheelies was good exercise and far better than simply mooching about or sitting on a bench. But today I was quite glad that we were just going to mooch as it meant I could break the news without having to make a big thing of it and frighten Frizz.

"D'you know," I said, as we ambled off in the sunshine, "I'm absolutely annoyed!"

I waited for someone to ask me why, but at that moment a group of Year Fours rushed past screaming. One of them bashed into Keri, who yelled, "Watch where you're going, can't you!"

"Honestly," she grumbled. "They have *no* manners, these people!"

Lily did a little hop and skip, then twirled in a circle. Lily can do things like that, and it doesn't make you want to cringe. Unlike Jessamy. Jessamy is just embarrassing!

"Poor things," I said. "They are only young!"

"Old enough to know better," snarled Keri, rubbing her ankle. "They shouldn't be allowed to rampage like that."

"Ram-*page*!" cried Lily. She took off, in a great leap. "Ram-*page*, ram-*page*, ram-*page*!"

We watched for a while in silence as Lily leaped and pranced.

"D'you know," I said, again, "I am most tremendously annoyed."

"Ram-p-p-PAGE!" Lily screeched to a halt in front of me.

"Did you say you were annoyed?"

"Yes, I am," I said. "Hugely!"

"Why? What's happened?"

"I've got to go and take this stupid entrance exam!"

"What?" Keri stopped rubbing her ankle. "What are you talking about? What entrance exam?"

"For the High School."

"Polly!" Frizz turned a stricken face towards me. "You're not going to the *High* School?"

"No way!" I said. "I'm just taking the exam."

"Why take the exam if you're not going there?" said Keri.

"'Cos I can't get out of it! My parents went and

arranged it without asking me."

"But didn't you tell them?" wailed Frizz. "Didn't you tell them that we're all going to Heathfield? That we swore an oath?"

"I did," I said. "I told them!"

"What did they say?"

"Mum just went on about the High School being all girls and having smaller classes."

"And wearing a yucky uniform." Keri made a being-sick noise.

"Yeeurgh!"

"Yeeurgh," I said.

"Groo," went Lily, standing on one leg and sticking the other up in the air. "Actually, they have uniforms at Rosemount."

"Yes, but it doesn't matter there," said Keri. "That's not an ordinary sort of school."

I couldn't honestly see what difference this was supposed to make, but I assured Keri that I wouldn't be wearing the yucky High School uniform because I wasn't going to go there.

"I'm just taking the exam! I'm not going to pass it."

"So why take it?" wailed Frizz.

"Because I can't get out of it! They've filled in the forms. They did it without even asking me. But I'll never get a scholarship! It's just a total waste of time."

"Well, so *that's* all right," said Keri. "I must say, it seems a bit stupid, bothering to take the exam if you're not going to go there, but parents do have these weird ideas. Like one time my mum was talking about sending me to boarding school. Can you imagine?"

I said, "*Boarding* school?"

"Yes, 'cos she went to one. She says it's character-forming."

"I would *die* if I had to go to boarding school," said Frizz.

"Really?" Keri studied her a moment, as if she was some kind of strange insect that had crawled out from under a stone. "I think it would be quite fun, actually. Apart from not being with you guys, natch! But then my dad said they didn't have the money to send me *and* my brothers, and they have to go 'cos they're boys."

We all made loud groaning noises.

"That is so sexist!" said Lily.

"My dad is sexist," said Keri. "He's the most sexist person I know. He doesn't think they should have women in the army."

We groaned again, even more loudly than before.

"As for girls playing *football*," said Keri. She rolled her eyes.

"He says that is the end of civilisation as he knows it."

"What about boxing?" I said.

"Oh, pur-*lease*! Mum says don't even talk about it, it'll give him a heart attack."

"Wow!" said Lily.

"Well, at least it means you'll be coming with us to Heathfield," I said.

"Yes! Worse luck."

"Don't you *want* to come to Heathfield?" said Frizz.

"I'd sooner go to boarding school! I mean—" Keri's eyes roved around the playground and came to rest on Jessamy. Showing off, as usual. Doing the splits in front of an admiring crowd. "I'd sooner go *anywhere*," said Keri, "than be stuck with her!"

"Who wouldn't?" I said.

We didn't talk any more about me taking the entrance exam, and I was really relieved as it was something I just wanted to push to the back of my mind and not think about. I did notice that Frizz was doing rather a lot of sighing, and heavy breathing, and kept giving me these sad, reproachful, sheepdoggy sort of looks, but I didn't say anything as I thought it best not. I mean, I didn't want to encourage her. Frizz does tend to get a bit mumpish about things. She is a terrible worrier.

I kind of hoped that by the end of the afternoon (if I took no notice) she might have found something else to fret about. Like, for instance, whether her left big toe was abnormal, which she had recently thought that it might be.

"Look!" she'd said, when I was sleeping over at her place during half term. "It's growing all crooked!"

I didn't mind her worrying about her big toe. She'd shown it to Lily and Keri in the playground and we'd all made jokes about it, like Keri had said maybe she'd end up walking sideways, like a crab, and Lily had done a funny crab dance, and even Frizz, in the end, had had to laugh.

So if she wanted to talk about her toe, and tell me that it was deformed and that it would probably have to be cut off and she'd have to have a false one, that was OK. I'd talk about it. What I didn't want to talk about was me taking the entrance exam!

But Frizz had obviously been brooding all day. "What happens if you pass?" she said, as we walked down the hill at the end of school. She looked at me with her sad, reproachful, sheepdoggy look. "You'll go the High School and I'll be left on my own with Keri!"

"It's not going to happen," I said. "I told you! I'd have to get a scholarship."

"But suppose you do?"

"I won't! I'm not clever enough."

"You are clever," said Frizz. "You're a boffin!"

I said, "I am not a boffin! My brother's a boffin. Not me!"

Frizz refused to be comforted. She moaned on about it all the way down the hill. I got a bit irritated, to tell the truth. Sometimes Frizz can get you like this. I know she can't help it, but honestly! It wasn't my fault I was having to take the stupid exam. I hadn't asked to. I'd said all along I didn't want to.

I said this to Frizz, and she munched at her lip for a while and then muttered, "Sorry. I know you can't help it."

"Well, I can't," I said. "You have to do what your mum and dad tell you." Then I had a sudden idea. "Maybe you could take the exam, as well!"

Frizz turned this tragic face on me. No one can look more tragic than Frizz!

"What's the point?" she said. "I'd *never* get a scholarship!"

"Well, I'm not going to, either," I said. "Know why?"

64

Slowly, Frizz shook her head.

"'Cos I'm going to make sure that I don't!"

Frizzle's eyes widened. "How?"

"I'm going to fail on purpose," I said.

"Fail on *purpose*?"

I nodded.

"But what about your mum and dad?"

"They won't know. They'll think I just wasn't clever enough. Which I'm not, anyway!"

Frizz opened her mouth. "You —"

I cut her off, quick as could be.

"Spit in your hand," I said.

"Do what?" said Frizz.

"Spit in your hand!"

"What for?"

"Just do it!"

Frizz crinkled her forehead but obediently spat, and so did I. Then I dipped my finger first into her spit, then into mine, and solemnly licked it.

"Now I've taken an oath," I said. "So I've got to fail!"

Chapter 6

The day of the exam arrived and Mum and me drove into town, to the High School.

"If you get in," burbled Mum, all merry and happy, "you'll be able to go on the bus with Craig."

Oh, I thought, *bliss*. To go on the bus, with Craig! I'd seen boys from Craig's school on the bus. They all swarmed on to the top deck and roared about amongst the seats, bellowing and bawling and giving their loud honking laughs. I didn't want to go on the bus with Craig!

Anyway, I wouldn't be because I wasn't going to

get in. I'd taken an oath!

Mum parked the car in the school car park, in one of the bays marked VISITORS. There were some steps leading up to a front door, with a big notice saying EXAM CANDIDATES THIS WAY. Mum went first, and I followed, with a sinking heart. Dad had said to me, over breakfast: "Well, Poll Doll! So it's the big day, eh?"

Gloomily, I had agreed that it was.

"Don't look so worried," said Dad. "You either get in or you don't. No big deal. Just look at it as a bit of fun."

"Day off school," said Craig.

But I would ever so much rather have been sitting in class with Keri and Lily and Frizz, the same as usual.

As he left for the bus, Craig thrust an envelope at me. Inside the envelope was a good luck card, with a black cat, and *Lotsa luv XXX Craig*.

I went, "Gulp!"

"Isn't that nice?" beamed Mum. "What a nice thought!" She told me that it had been entirely his own idea. "I didn't put him up to it!"

That just made it worse. There was me, planning to fail on purpose, and there was my horrible brother being nice as pie and giving me good luck cards! And

Mum and Dad, all beaming and hopeful.

Just for a minute I felt what I think are known as *qualms*. An odd word! Meaning that I got collywobbles in the pit of my stomach and wondered if I could go through with it. Failing on purpose, that is. Of course I would *fail*. But maybe I could just fail naturally, without having to try?

I'd never get a scholarship! That was for sure.

"Well, here it is," said Mum, when we reached the High School. "Don't you think it would be lovely to go here?"

I made this mumbling sound. I could see that Mum was impressed! The High School is this old, old, very ancient building that used to be somebody's palace about a millennium ago. Well, centuries ago. It is of historical interest and people come from all over to look at it. In the holidays there are guided tours. But this wasn't holidays and at the time Mum and me got there the corridors were swarming with girls all wearing green kilts and waistcoats (some had sweaters) which is the uniform that Keri said was yucky and that we had both gone "Yeeurgh!" just thinking of.

"Don't they look smart?" said Mum.

Inside myself I went "Yeeurgh!" because I knew

that was what Keri would expect of me, but to please Mum I nodded and said "Mm!" as brightly as I could. As a matter of fact, they did look quite smart. I mean, dead naff, *of course*; but kind of cute, all the same.

Before sitting the exam I had to go in to see the headmistress for my interview. Most people had already had theirs; there was just me and one other girl. We sat there in the waiting room, with our mums, not speaking. I peeped across at the other girl from under my lashes, trying not to let her see. She wasn't hugely pretty; in fact, not really pretty at all. More like…fascinating. She had this tiny face, shaped like a triangle, with a small but rather pointy nose and sticky-out teeth, with a brace. And her hair was really crazy! Cut short and ragged. All in spikes and spokes. All over the place. Totally mad! But it made you want to look at her.

She wasn't wearing any school uniform that I could recognise, and this was explained when her mum and mine got talking, in the way that mums do. They started swopping information, and the other mum said that they had travelled all the way up from the south coast. She said they were moving to the district very shortly, and "We're really keen for Chloë to come here. We've heard such good things about the school!"

Mum at once said how it was top of the lists, and noted for its academic achievements, and me and the girl, Chloë, exchanged these glances. I pulled a face and Chloë giggled, which at once made me feel better. Up until then I had been suffering from what Mum calls the heeby jeebies, meaning butterflies and collywobbles and things that go "blurp!" deep inside you. It wasn't the exam that was bothering me, it was the interview.

The school secretary came in and said, "Polly Roberts?" and Mum gave me a little push and whispered, "Off you go! Nothing to be scared of." But she wasn't the one it was happening to!

The headmistress wasn't old and frumpy as I'd thought she'd be. Her name was Mrs Kershaw, and she had dark curly hair and wore make-up and nail polish and *trousers*! I couldn't believe it! The headmistress at our school, Mrs Cuthbert, is plump and grey-haired and wears cardies and flowery skirts. Mrs Cuthbert would never wear trousers! Of course, she does have quite a big bottom. But all the little ones love her and go to her for cuddles. I couldn't quite see anyone going to Mrs Kershaw for a cuddle, though maybe you're not expected to in senior school.

She smiled at me, and I smiled back, as brightly as I could, showing all my teeth. And then I thought that perhaps that might make it seem like I wasn't taking things seriously enough, so I pulled my lips down and tried to look solemn. Which wasn't difficult 'cos I was feeling dead nervous!

The thing that really bothered me was in case she asked why I wanted to come to the High School, because then what would I say? You are always supposed to tell the truth, but she might be angry and tell me to go away and stop wasting her time, and poor Mum would be *so* upset.

Fortunately, however, she didn't ask me. Instead she wanted to know things like which were my favourite subjects at school (to which I said English, Art and History) and what sort of things did I like doing out of school (to which I said reading, playing with Bundle, and staying over with Frizz). She also asked me if I was a sporty type (to which I said no, because of always telling the truth) and how I would feel about homework.

I said that we did homework now – "A little bit." Mrs Kershaw said I would have to do a lot if I came to the High School, and I said (being truthful) that I wouldn't mind. I thought afterwards that perhaps I should have recoiled in horror and gone "Ugh! No!" or told her that I *hated* homework. Something like that. Then she would immediately have put a black mark against my name and have told Mum that she didn't think I was a suitable candidate.

But Mum was ever so excited and it would have seemed a bit mean, so on the whole I was glad that I hadn't said it. I was still going to fail the exam!

We had to wait while Chloë was being interviewed as the exam didn't start for another half an hour. Very nerve-racking! (Even if I was going to fail.) While we were waiting Mum made me tell her everything that Mrs Kershaw had asked me, and everything that I had said in reply.

"Well! It doesn't sound as if it went too badly." She beamed at me. "How do you feel?"

"All right," I mumbled.

"Now, Polly, just remember," said Mum, "it's *fun*. That's all! Just fun."

She and Dad kept saying that. They didn't want me to be disappointed if I didn't get in! I thought, "They are the ones that are going to be disappointed", and just for a moment I felt a terrible pang of guilt; but only for a moment. After all, I'd *told* Mum I didn't want to go there! I'd told her I wanted to go to

Heathfield. And anyway, I'd sworn an oath.

Chloë came back from her interview and the secretary said it was time for us to go and take the exam. Our two mums went off together. Mum said she was going to do some shopping and I wished that I could go with her.

The exam was held in a big hall. There were hundreds of desks, all set out in rows, with people sitting at them. At least a hundred. Well, maybe about eighty. Well, anyway, a LOT. It made me feel better, because I thought that if there were all those people trying for a scholarship I stood absolutely *no* chance of getting one. Maybe I wouldn't have to fail on purpose!

The first paper was Arithmetic, which is not my best subject. Mr Francis, one of our teachers, said to me in Year Four that I was the only person he knew who could add two and two and make them come to five. I think he was joking! But only sort of.

There was lots of stuff I just knew I'd got wrong in the Arithmetic paper. I thought probably they would take one look and say, "Oh, we cannot have this moron child in the school," and that made me feel that I needn't have bothered to take an oath. I was far too stupid even to pass the exam! No one would ever give me a scholarship.

The next paper was General, and again there were loads of things I didn't know and loads of things I just had to guess at; but in any case, once they'd finished marking my Arithmetic paper I reckoned they wouldn't bother marking anything else. They would say, "This girl is just too dumb for words", and would feel insulted at the mere thought of me ever putting on their yucky green uniform.

Last of all, we came to English. I'd had this idea that what I'd do, I'd muddle up all my nouns and verbs, and I'd deliberately spell things wrong. I'd forget about *i before e except after c*, and I wouldn't bother with commas or full stops, and also I'd make my handwriting really bad. But English is my favourite subject! And they wanted us to write a poem, and I just love to write poems! There was a choice of subjects, and the one I chose was *Home*.

This is the poem that I wrote:

"Home is where my mum and dad are,
Home is where my brother is.
Home is Bundle, he's my dog.
Home is everything I love.

"Home is humble, just a house
Stuck between two other houses.
It is not grand or rich or big,
But it's where I love to live."

Actually it went on for eight more verses!!! I do tend to get a bit carried away when I write poems.

I started off thinking that I would do it *badly*. I thought it would be fun! I wrote:

"Hom is were my mum and dad is
Hom is were my bruthr is"

Making my writing all scratchy and horrible. And then, all of a sudden, I just couldn't bear it! I snatched up my black felt-tip pen and blotched it all out and started over again. I forgot about Frizzle, I forgot about my oath, I just wrote and wrote, and went on writing. I was still writing when the bell rang and we all had to finish. I just had time to do my last two lines:

"Home is safe as safe can be
Home means all the world to me."

And then the teacher said, "Pens down," and we all came to a stop.

Chloë screwed her face up in a grimace as we filed out of the hall.

"See you in Heaven!" she said.

I couldn't work out what she meant. Did she mean, see you in September? Like she really thought she'd get a scholarship, and so would I. Or did she mean Heaven like Heaven when you die, and she *didn't* think she'd get a scholarship? I couldn't decide!

Mum was waiting eagerly for me in the car.

"So, how did you get on?" she said.

I told her that I'd got on OK in English – "I wrote a poem" – but that I'd done *really* badly in Arithmetic and not very well in General.

"There were all these questions I didn't know how to answer," I said. "And I just know I got most of the Arithmetic wrong!"

"Well, never mind," said Mum. I could tell she was disappointed, and was pretending not to be. "You did your best, you can't do more. And who knows? It might have been a lot better than you imagine!"

It better hadn't be, I thought. I'd sworn an oath! I'd given Frizzle my word.

"I think it was bad," I said.

"Polly, don't torture yourself," said Mum. "It doesn't matter. Let's go and have some tea!"

Chapter 7

Everybody wanted to know how I'd got on! Almost the minute we got home the telephone rang and it was my gran. Gran had also sent me a good luck card. (So had two of my aunties, and my cousin Jenna, and my other gran, and Mr Deacon that lives next door! Fortunately, they didn't *all* ring.)

"How did it go?" asked Gran.

I told her what I'd told Mum, that I had done *really* badly on General and really *really* badly on Arithmetic.

"I wrote a good poem," I said. "But I don't understand about fractions!"

"Never mind," said Gran, comfortably. "Neither do I, and I've had sixty years to get my head round them!"

"But I also didn't know lots of questions in the General Knowledge," I said.

"Pet, don't worry," said Gran.

I wasn't worried! The more I thought about it, the less worried I became. I was *never* going to get a scholarship! I was just trying to prepare Mum and Dad. I knew they'd be disappointed, no matter what they said.

At half past four, Craig came roaring in.

"How'd it go? Have you got in?"

I crinkled my nose and said, "No way!" at the same time as Mum, laughing, said, "Give her a chance! She's only just taken the exam. It'll be a week before we hear."

"I heard immediately," boasted Craig.

"No, you did not!" said Mum. "You sat the exam and went back later for your interview. That was when you heard."

"Yes, and you had *collywobbles*," I said. "I remember!"

I took Bundle round the block, and on the way back Mr Deacon popped his head out of the front door and said, "Well, young Polly! How did it go?"

"Not very well," I said. "I didn't understand the fractions."

"Fractions?" said Mr Deacon. "You're still doing fractions? I thought it was all decimal, these days."

"Decimal fractions," I said.

"Oh! Decimal fractions." Mr Deacon shook his head. "You've got me there!" He chuckled. "I'm afraid I'd never get a scholarship!"

"Me neither," I said.

At six o'clock, Dad came home. He said, "Hi, Poll Doll! How did it go?"

I didn't tell Dad about not understanding fractions as he has spent hours and hours trying to explain them to me. Dad is good at numbers. He has to be. He puts in swimming pools for people, and has to work out complicated things to do with the amount of water. If I ever put in a swimming pool for someone it would be a DISASTER! All the water would flow over and flood the garden. It might even flood the whole street. I just wouldn't know where to begin.

So anyway, I told Dad that I didn't think I'd done very well, and Dad put his arm around me and said, "Don't be downhearted. Let's wait and see! You might be surprised."

"I'll never get a scholarship," I said. "There were nearly a hundred people there!"

I'd counted them while I was trying to work out some stupid question about marbles. Like, if you have thirty marbles and you lose 0.3 of them, how many have you lost? My brain just seized up, and instead of counting marbles I started counting people.

"There were *eighty-three*," I said. "And they only give two scholarships!"

"Oh, Polly, not all eighty-three of you were trying for a scholarship," said Mum. "Is that what you thought?"

I nodded, uncertainly.

"Most people were just sitting the entrance exam. I should think probably only about…oh, I don't know! About a quarter of you, maybe, were trying for scholarships."

"That's still a lot," I said.

"'Tisn't!" said Craig. "It's only ten and a bit for each one."

Yes, I thought, but probably all the other ten and a bit could understand fractions. They had probably answered the marble question. *And* the one about baked beans that hadn't made any sense.

"Don't let him wind you up," said Dad. "We told you before, it's no big deal."

"She wrote a lovely poem," said Mum. "Polly! Tell Dad your poem. Tell him how it ended."

I recited the last two lines:

"Home is safe as safe can be
Home means all the world to me"

and Dad hugged me and said, "That's my girl! Who cares about scholarships?"

We'd just finished tea when the telephone rang. This time, it was Frizz.

"Polly!" she said. "How did you get on?"

I thought that I would scream if anyone else asked me that question. But I knew that Frizz was anxious.

"No need to worry," I said. I cupped my hand over the mouthpiece and whispered, "I did what I said."

"Did you really?" said Frizz. "*Really?*"

"Yes, I did," I said, "really!"

"But w—"

"Look, I can't talk now," I said. "I'll tell you tomorrow!"

Guess what? First thing that happens when I get into school next morning…

"Well, Polly!" says our class teacher, Mrs Arkle. "And how did you get on yesterday?"

You can't really scream at your class teacher. So I just made a little grimace and said, "I didn't do very well on the Arithmetic."

"It is your weakest subject," agreed Mrs Arkle. "But you'll have done well in English!"

Frizz was there, and heard this.

"*Did* you?" she hissed, as we went over to our table. "Did you really do well in English?"

"Yes, but I messed up on everything else," I said. "Tell you later!"

So later on, in the playground, I told them about all the questions I hadn't been able to answer and all the questions I hadn't understood and all the questions I'd thought about since and knew that I'd got wrong.

"Like what, for instance?" said Keri.

"Well!" I giggled. "I got Madrid and Madras muddled up... I said that Madrid was in Spain!"

There was a silence.

"Isn't it?" said Frizz.

"Certainly was last I heard," said Keri. "Of course, it may have moved. Strange things do happen."

"It hasn't moved," said Lily. "It's still there."

They all three looked at me like I was some kind of traitor.

"I didn't do it on purpose!" I said.

"No. Well. All right," said Keri. "Tell us something else you got wrong!"

"Almost *all* of the Arithmetic," I said.

"Give us a f'r' instance!"

"F'r' instance… I said that an eighth was smaller than a quarter!"

"Which it is," said Keri.

"What?" I stared at her. "How can it be?"

"If you cut things into four and you cut things into eight," said Keri, "the things that have been cut into eight are going to be smaller than the things that have been cut into four. Right?"

"Right." Lily nodded. "Stands to reason."

"Oh. Well! There was this question about marbles," I said, "that I couldn't even *do*. And then there was one about baked beans that I didn't even *understand*. And then there was all this stuff about shading things in, and changing something from ordinary fractions into decimals, and then" – I rolled my eyes – "there was *subtraction*."

"Subtraction's easy," said Keri.

"*Decimal* subtraction."

"Even easier!"

"It might be for you," I said. "I never know where to put the dot!"

Comfortingly, as we walked back into school, I told Frizzle that there had been eighty-three people taking the exam. I didn't tell her they weren't all trying for a scholarship. Frizz said, "*Eighty-three*?" sounding suitably awed.

"Yes, and they only give two scholarships," I said.

Later, while we were having silent reading, Frizz pushed a piece of paper at me. She'd obviously been doing sums.

"*That's forty-one and a half for each scollership!*"

I swallowed, and nodded. Frizz widened her eyes.

"*I won't get one!*" I wrote.

"I hope you don't," worried Frizz, on the way home.

"I won't," I said. "I told you!"

"I don't know what I'd do," wailed Frizz, "if I had to go to Heathfield on my own!"

I said, "You wouldn't be on your own, you'd be with Keri."

"It wouldn't be the same!"

"It'd be better than being on your own," I said, "wouldn't it?"

Frizz didn't say anything to this. She just scrunched her lips and did this draggy thing with her feet, scuffing her toes into the pavement as we walked.

"Wouldn't it?" I said.

Frizz humped a shoulder.

"Well, anyway," I said, "it's not going to happen. Watch my lips…it is NOT GOING TO HAPPEN!"

But then… Oh, grief! Oh, woe! One day I got home and it had come. THE LETTER. It had arrived that morning, after I'd gone to school. Mum had been sitting on it all day! Of course I don't mean that literally. But she hadn't opened it 'cos of waiting for me.

"It didn't seem fair," she said. "After all, it's your letter, really. Here! You open it and we'll read it together."

Slowly, I slit open the envelope. Slowly, I took out the sheet of paper. Slowly, I unfolded it.

Mum said, "Don't be nervous! Just remember…if you haven't got in, it's not the end of the world."

I swallowed. I couldn't help being nervous! But not for the reason Mum thought.

I got as far as "Dear Mr & Mrs Roberts" when Mum, who was looking over my shoulder, suddenly gave a great screech.

"Polly! You've done it! You're in!"

Chapter 8

I just couldn't believe it.

"Polly" Mum clasped me to her in a big bear hug. "You clever girl! Just wait till your dad hears. I must go and ring your gran!"

She rang both my grans. Big Gran and little Gran. They both went, "Oh, Polly! What a clever girl!"

Then Craig came home. He took one look at Mum's face, which was like a big banana split, and went, "What is it? Is it the scholarship? Have you got one? I knew you would! What did I tell you? Easy peasy!"

"It wasn't easy peasy at *all*," I said.

"No, it wasn't," said Mum. "It was quite a struggle, wasn't it, Poll? But she did it! Oh, I must pop next door and tell Mr Deacon. He'll be so thrilled!"

She grabbed me by the arm and whizzed me round to Mr Deacon's.

"Wonderful news," she said, when Mr Deacon shuffled to the door. "She did it! She's got a scholarship!"

"Well, bless my buttons," said Mr Deacon. "I'm living next door to a genius. And that's in spite of decimal fractions!"

"I just know I got them all wrong," I said. "It was this poem I wrote. That's what did it."

"English is way her best subject," beamed Mum. "Craig's more into science, but Poll's like her mum... She's a word person."

So Mum and the word person went zizzing back indoors and Mum flung open the fridge and said, "Look!" and pointed to a huge enormous chocolate cake, one of her extra specially gorgeously gooey ones with about ten centimetres of icing on the top and a thick squiggly layer in the middle. She brought it out and showed it to us.

"I made it this morning, just in case... I thought if

you didn't get in, it would be a consolation prize. But you have! So now I'm going to finish it off!" And in little silver balls she spelt out WELL DONE POLLY all across it.

"Yummy," I said.

"You deserve it," said Mum.

"What's this?" Craig had been rootling about in the fridge. He yanked out a bottle. "Is this *booze*?"

"Champagne," said Mum. "Don't shake it!" she shrieked.

"It's pink," I said. I was remembering Keri and her remarks about pink knickers. But I guess pink champagne is different!

While we were waiting for Dad to come home, Mum rang up just about everybody she could think of, which was all five of my aunties; three of her friends; our next door neighbour where we used to live before we lived where we live now; and the lady in the local bookshop. I don't know why she rang the lady in the bookshop. She was just so excited!

"I was telling her about it," said Mum. "She asked me to be sure and let her know."

Mum could hardly wait for Dad to come in! I couldn't wait, either, mainly because I wanted to start eating chocolate cake, but also because I was happy that Mum was happy, and happy that Dad was going to be happy. It is nice when your mum and dad are happy, especially when you're the one that's made them be! I personally was still reeling from the shock. I kept thinking, "This can't be true! This can't be happening!" How could I go to the High School, all by myself, without the others? And even worse, how was I going to tell them??? Frizz, in particular. I just couldn't think how I was going to break it to her.

At last we heard Dad's key in the door. Mum gave me a little push.

"Go on! Go and tell him!"

"You do it," I said.

"No! Don't be silly," said Mum; and she bundled me out into the hall.

"Dad," I said.

"What?" Dad twitched an eyebrow. "You been up to something? You're looking guilty!"

"I got the scholarship," I said.

Oh, wow! Dad picked me up and swung me round and hugged me so hard he nearly squeezed all the air out of me. He was, like, demented!

"I told you she'd get one," said Craig. "Can we start eating, now? And can I have some booze, please?"

I had a vast slice of chocolate cake and just a teensy little glass of the lovely pink champagne, which although it looked so lovely, didn't taste all that nice, to be honest. But I drank it because Craig was drinking it and I didn't want to be left out. I mean, it was my celebration, not his!

"Aren't you glad, now, that we made you take the exam?" said Mum. "Aren't you excited?"

I was getting to be. Maybe it was just the pink fizzy stuff! Or maybe it was because Mum and Dad were so excited. But I couldn't help feeling just a little bit proud of myself. All those people, and I'd got a scholarship! You would have to be an angel or something not to feel just a tiny bit pleased. Well, that is what I would think.

I am not an angel!!! But I still wondered how I was going to tell Frizz.

"You're not worried about Dawn, are you?" said Mum. Sometimes Mum seems to have that thing where she can read what I am thinking.

"We were going to Heathfield together," I mumbled.

"Oh, Polly, I know you were," said Mum. "But it's not as if she'll be on her own! There'll be loads of people going there from your school. She'll be all right! You're the one who'll be on your own."

I must have given Mum what she calls my "dying duck" look because she at once put an arm round me and hugged me to her and said, "Cheer up! You'll soon make friends. Maybe that nice girl Chloë will be there?"

"It won't be the same without the others," I muttered.

"No, it won't," agreed Mum. "But the fact is, Poll, sooner or later you'd probably all grow apart, anyway."

"We wouldn't!" I looked at Mum, reproachfully. What a thing to say! "Why should we?" I said.

"Well, you are all very different," said Mum. "You'd find you were probably making new friends and moving on even if you did go to Heathfield."

"I would *not*!" I shouted. "And I won't, not ever!"

I thought it was so mean of Mum to say that. I made up my mind that first thing next morning I would have to be brave and call a secret meeting and break the news, and me and Frizz – and Lily and Keri – would swear our oath all over again. However…

Things don't always work out the way you plan. First off, I arrived at school late on account of Dad saying he was going that way and would give me a lift. *Not* a good idea, as it turned out. We ran into a huge traffic jam, as a result of which I raced huffing and puffing into class just as Mrs Arkle was about to start taking the register. I plonked myself down next to Frizz, who immediately started to whisper at me.

"Secret meeting…first break."

I said, "What? Why?"

"Dunno," said Frizz. "Ask Keri."

I swizzled round in my chair and mouthed, "What are we meeting for?" but Keri just mouthed back, "Tell you later!"

At break time we all rushed to our secret place and crammed ourselves in.

"Well," said Keri, "Have I got news for you! Guess what? I'm going to go to boarding school, after all!"

We gaped at her, our jaws dropping.

"I didn't want to," she said. "I argued like crazy! But you know what it's like when your mum and dad get an idea into their heads."

I nodded, glumly. I knew!

"I thought you said your dad said only your brothers could go?" said Lily.

"He did! I thought I was safe! But then my godmother went and offered to pay the fees." Keri rolled her eyes. "Without even *asking* me!"

"They don't ever ask you," I said. They pretend to, but in the end you always have to do what they want.

"*Boarding* school," said Frizz.

"It's not as bad as it sounds. It's only weekly. I'll still be home at weekends. I can see you all then."

"I would just die," said Frizz.

"Me, too," I said. And then, ever so ever so quickly, before I could get cold feet, I gabbled, "I've got something to tell, too… I've gone and got a scholarship!"

Frizz let out a loud howl. "I knew you would! I said you were a boffin!"

"I'm not," I said. "I'm not a boffin! I got so many things wrong you just wouldn't believe. It was my poem that did it."

"You'll have to wear that yucky uniform," said Keri.

"Yes, I *know*," I said. "Groo!" I added.

"Double groo," said Keri. "Green kilts. Puke!"

"We swore an oath." Frizz looked at me, accusingly. "We said we'd all go to Heathfield!"

"Actually," said Lily. She sounded a bit apologetic. "*Actually*, we didn't. What we *actually* swore—" She fished in her bag and pulled out a tatty piece of paper. "We swear to stay together, all the time we're still at school. For better or for worse, 'cos that's our rule. That's what we *actually* swore."

"So how can we be together if we're all at different places?" wailed Frizz.

"We can always meet at weekends."

"We'll have *stacks* of things to talk about," said Keri.

"And we can still sleep over," I said.

Frizz sniffed dolefully. "I'm going to be stuck all by myself with that hideous Jessamy!"

I felt so bad about it. I felt almost worse about that than anything else. Leaving poor old Frizz at the mercy of that dreadful girl!

"I'm really sorry," I whispered. "I just wish there was something I could do!"

"We could try putting a hex on her," said Lily. "Maybe her mum and dad will emigrate to Australia."

"Yes, and take her with them!"

"I should be so lucky," said Frizz.

She spent the rest of the morning in a limp heap. I tried to avoid looking at her. Her eyes were all big and moist and kind of...*soulful*.

In the playground during afternoon break, it came up to me. That Girl. *Her. Jessamy.*

"Hey!" she said, poking at me. "I hear you're

going to the High School?"

I wondered how she had found out, but like I say, nothing stays secret for very long at our school. Lily and Keri must have gone round telling people.

I said, "Mm."

"She's got a scholarship," said Frizz.

Jessamy tossed her hair. "She's a boffin!" She made it sound like being a boffin is like being something stinky that's crawled out of a drain. "I haven't got a scholarship, 'cos I don't need one, but I'm going there too!"

There was a startled silence.

"You?" said Keri.

"I didn't see you at the entrance exam," I said.

"I took it earlier," said Jessamy. "I took it *weeks* ago, only I didn't tell anyone in case I didn't get in. I never thought I would! But my Arithmetic paper was so brilliant, it was one of the best ones they've ever had, I got *ninety-eight per cent*! What did you get?"

"Haven't the foggiest," I said. "About minus ten, I should think."

"But you wrote a *genius* poem," urged Keri.

"I wrote a good poem, too," said Jessamy.

I looked at her with distaste. "I thought you were

going to Heathfield to be on their gym team?"

"I was," gurgled Jessamy.

"So won't they be expecting you?"

She hunched a shoulder. "Too bad! They'll just have to do without me."

"That'll break their hearts," said Keri.

"Well, it probably will," agreed Jessamy. "But the High School has an even better team!"

Oh, that girl! She is so horrible. And now I was the one that was going to be stuck with her!

"Poor you," said Lily, as Jessamy went cavorting back to her friends.

"Yuck uniform, school full of boffin heads, and Jessamy Jones…yeeurgh!" went Keri.

I hung my head. "It's like some kind of horrible torture!"

"Well, it serves you right," said Frizz. "I hope she makes your life a misery!"

I didn't mind her saying it. Not really. It was better than being all weepish and woebegone.

"We'll still be friends though, won't we?" said Lily.

Frizz sniffed, "Don't see how we can."

"Well, we can!" said Keri. "And we will! We'll always be friends." She looked at us, rather fiercely. "It's up to us!"

"Let's swear," I said.

"Yes! Swear!" said Lily. "Swear we'll always be friends!"

Lily stuck out a fist, with the thumb stuck up. Keri did the same, clamping on to Lily. Then I clamped on to Keri, and Frizz clamped on to me.

"Do it double, do it double!" urged Lily.

So we made another chain, on top of the first. Eight fists, all clamped together.

"Now swear," said Lily.

Solemnly, we swore.

"Friends for ever!"

"No matter what!"

"Lick your finger, hope to die—"

We all licked a finger and held it up in front of us.

"Lick your finger, hope to die,
Drop down dead if I tell a lie!"

"That's OK," said Lily. "That's as good as a blood oath, that is."

I think it made Frizz feel better. As we left school at the end of the day she hooked her arm through mine and whispered, "I didn't really mean what I said...'bout Jessamy making your life a misery."

"'S all right," I said.

"Just so long as we're always going to be friends," said Frizz.

"We are," I said. "We've sworn! All of us! Specially you and me. Friends for ever!"

Frizz gave me a little happy smile.

"Friends for ever!" she said.

About the Author

Jean Ure had her first book published while she was still at school and immediately went rushing out into the world declaring that she was AN AUTHOR. But it was another few years before she had her second book published, and during that time she had to work at lots of different jobs to earn money. In the end she went to drama school to train as an actress. While she was there she met her husband and wrote another book. She has now written more than eighty books! She lives in Croydon with her husband and their family of seven rescued dogs and four rescued cats.

Girlfriends

Find out whether the Gang of Four stay friends for ever in the next book in the series!

1 84121 839 1 £3.99

Chapter 1

Starting at a new school is definitely scary. Especially when you don't know anyone. Then it is *double* scary!

A week ago I'd gone with Mum to buy my uniform. I wasn't scared then. I was excited! The High School uniform is green kilts and waistcoats, or sweaters for when it's cold. Keri says that all uniforms are naff, and that the High School uniform is one of the naffest. I don't agree! I know that Keri is our Style Queen, and dead cool, and buys all her gear from this mega-trendy store called Go Girl that I have almost never got anything from, as Mum says it is way too expensive and she is not forking out a week's wages for something I will grow out of before she has time to turn round, but I *don't care*. I just happen to think that green kilts and waistcoats are neat. So there!

Anyway. We bought the uniform and as soon as I got home I tried it all on again – just in case they'd given us the wrong size, or something; it's always best to check – and Mum yelled upstairs, "Polly! Come down and show Mr Deacon!" So I went next door and did a bit of a twizzle for Mr Deacon who is old as old but still takes an interest in what me and Craig are up to.

Then Mum wanted to take photos to send to my grans, and then Dad arrived and said, "Hey, get a load of that! Give us a twirl then!" and as I was twirling Craig came clumping through the door, took one look and went, "Yuckaroony! Green grollies!"

He can talk! His school has purple blazers with *bright yellow stripes*! That is yuckaroony, if anything is. They look like piles of vomit, going down the road.

I said this to him, and Mum said, "Polly and Craig! Stop being so disgusting." But it is the way we talk to each other. We do it all the time. (Craig is my brother and older than me by eighteen months, though quite honestly he is so childish it is just unbelievable.)

I spent the whole of that week trying on my new uniform. I love it to bits! Frizz came round and wanted to see me in it. She said in wistful tones that she wished she could have a uniform like that. "Black is so grungy."

Black is what they wear at Heathfield.

"But green *kilts*," I said. "It's a bit yucky!"

"I don't think it's yucky," said Frizz. "I think it's nice."

I reminded her that Keri had said it was dead naff. Frizz said, "Oh! Well. Keri."

I must admit that I giggled when she said this. As a rule we all agree, Frizz and me and Lily, that Keri is just so-o-o-o cool.

"Gives herself these airs and graces," said Frizz.

That is not at all a Frizz-type phrase. I reckon she'd heard her mum say it. Mums tend to think that Keri is a bit *too* cool. They would like us to stay ten years old for ever!

All week long I peacocked about in my uniform, trying it in all different ways. First with the waistcoat, then with the sweater. Then with the skirt normal length, then rolled over at the waist. Then with black tights, then with green. You can wear either. (But not brown, for some reason. Maybe Mrs Kershaw, the Headmistress, has a thing about it.)

By Monday, which was the start of term, I was feeling quite used to my lovely green uniform. But now I was all shaky and scared about going somewhere new. I had hordes of butterflies swarming in my stomach. I could feel them, fluttering and flitting. Suddenly I wished more than anything that I was going to Heathfield, with Frizz. I wished Mum and Dad had never made me sit the scholarship. I wished I'd never passed.

I'd secretly been a bit proud when I'd first heard. I'd

been a bit puffed up. Poor old Frizz, I'd thought, stuck at Heathfield! Boring black uniform. Huge classes. *Boys*. But at least Frizz would know people. There were loads of them going there from our old school. Practically half the class! And Lily was starting at Rosemount, which was where she'd always dreamed of going, and it wouldn't matter that she wouldn't know anyone because nobody else would either. They would all be new together. People come from all over, to go to Rosemount. It is a famous dance school and even has people from places such as Australia and Japan.

As for Keri, at her posh new boarding school, it wouldn't bother her one little bit. Keri isn't in the least shy. She just barges straight in and takes over. I wish I could be like that! But I am not, unfortunately. When I first meet people I am rather silly and turned in on myself.

I expect probably this is where I ought to tell about us all. The four of us. Lily, Keri, Frizz and me. We've been friends since just about as long as I can remember. Since Reception! Well, we have known each other since Reception. Frizz and me started being best friends in Year Two, and Lily and Keri in Year Three. And then we all became best friends together. The Gang of Four! Lily 'n' Keri 'n' Frizzle 'n' me. Everybody knew us! Even the teachers. They knew we all sat together and did things together and stuck up for each other. When we left Juniors to go to different schools, we made this sacred solemn vow that we would stay friends for ever. Come what may, for better or for worse. We swore a special oath and sealed it with our own spit (instead of blood).

Mum apologised for not being able to come with me, that first morning. She said, "I'm really sorry, Pol! I would if I could, but we're so short-handed."

She meant at work. She does care work at a local home for old people. I assured her that I really didn't mind going by myself. To be honest, I thought it would be a bit babyish, turning up with your mum. I'd been going to suggest that she dropped me off half a block early so no one would see us!

"I'll be all right," I told her.

Read the rest of

Girls Stick Together!

to find out what happens next…

Jean Ure

Girls Are Groovy!

£3.99   1 84121 843 X

Frizz is behaving very strangely.

Polly is worried that Frizz hates her new school and feels lonely without the rest of the Gang of Four.

But is Frizz feeling left out, or is she the grooviest girl of all?

£3.99   1 84121 847 2

When Polly gets back from summer camp it
        seems that all her friends have grown up and
left her behind. Even Frizz is wearing a bra!
        And they keep inviting boys to their parties.

Polly hates boys.
    But will she decide they're OK in the end?

More Orchard Red Apples

☑ Pink Knickers Aren't Cool!	*Jean Ure*	1 84121 835 9
☑ Girls Stick Together!	*Jean Ure*	1 84121 839 1
☐ Girls Are Groovy!	*Jean Ure*	1 84121 843 x
☐ Boys Are OK!	*Jean Ure*	1 84121 847 2
☐ Do Not Read This Book	*Pat Moon*	1 84121 435 3
☐ What Howls at the Moon in Frilly Knickers?	*E. F. Smith*	1 84121 808 1
☐ The Poltergoose	*Michael Lawrence*	1 86039 836 7
☐ The Killer Underpants	*Michael Lawrence*	1 84121 713 1
☐ The Toilet of Doom	*Michael Lawrence*	1 84121 752 2
☐ The Fire Within	*Chris d'Lacey*	1 84121 533 3
☐ The Salt Pirates of Skegness	*Chris d'Lacey*	1 84121 539 2

All Girlfriends books priced at £3.99, all others £4.99

Orchard Red Apples are available from all good bookshops,
or can be ordered direct from the publisher:
Orchard Books, PO BOX 29, Douglas IM99 1BQ
Credit card orders please telephone 01624 836000
or fax 01624 837033
or e-mail: bookshop@enterprise.net for details.

To order please quote title, author and ISBN
and your full name and address.
Cheques and postal orders should be made payable to
'Bookpost plc.'
Postage and packing is FREE within the UK
(overseas customers should add £1.00 per book).

Prices and availability are subject to change